If I Could Give You Christmas

— Written by —
Lynn Plourde

— Illustrated by —
Jennifer L. Meyer

Disney • HYPERION

Los Angeles   New York

First Edition, September 2019
10 9 8 7 6 5 4 3 2
FAC-029191-19212
Printed in Malaysia

This book is set in 25-point Horley Old Style/Monotype
Designed by Trish Parcell

Library of Congress Cataloging-in-Publication Data
Names: Plourde, Lynn, author. • Meyer, Jennifer L., illustrator.
Title: If I could give you Christmas / by Lynn Plourde ; illustrated by Jennifer L. Meyer.
Description: First edition. • Los Angeles ; New York : Disney-Hyperion, 2019.
• Summary: As animals big and small prepare for Christmas by decorating
a tree, singing carols, and stashing surprises, they see that the most
important gift of the season is being together.
Identifiers: LCCN 2018022922 • ISBN 9781368002677
Subjects: • CYAC: Christmas—Fiction. • Animals—Fiction.
Classification: LCC PZ7.P724 If 2019 • DDC [E]—dc23
LC record available at https://lccn.loc.gov/2018022922

Reinforced binding
Visit www.DisneyBooks.com

For Bentley, one of our family's favorite gifts
—L.P.

May this book bring you much
happiness and many fun moments
—J.L.M.

If I could give you Christmas,

it would taste like the first falling snowflake.

If I could give you Christmas,
it would be the freshest,
pointiest, piney-est tree.

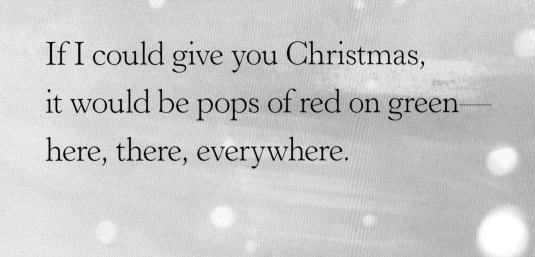

If I could give you Christmas,
it would be pops of red on green—
here, there, everywhere.

If I could give you Christmas,

it would sound like a chorus of chirping carolers.

If I could give you Christmas,

it would smell like
wafts and whiffs

of gingerbread and cocoa.

If I could give you Christmas,

it would be stashing secret surprises.

If I could give you Christmas,

it would be gliding, snow-white sliding.

If I could give you Christmas,
it would be wibbly-wobbly skating on a pond.

If I could give you Christmas,
it would be greeting friendly faces in the doorway.

If I could give you Christmas,
it would be a snuggly story time
under a giant night-light.

If I could give you Christmas,

it would be staying up extra late on Christmas Eve.

If I could give you Christmas,

it would be sharing the brightest twinkling star.

If I could give you Christmas,
it would be that tickly-tummy feeling
early on Christmas morn.

If YOU could give ME Christmas,
there's something you should know. . . .

My favorite gift at Christmas . . .

. . . doesn't have a bow.

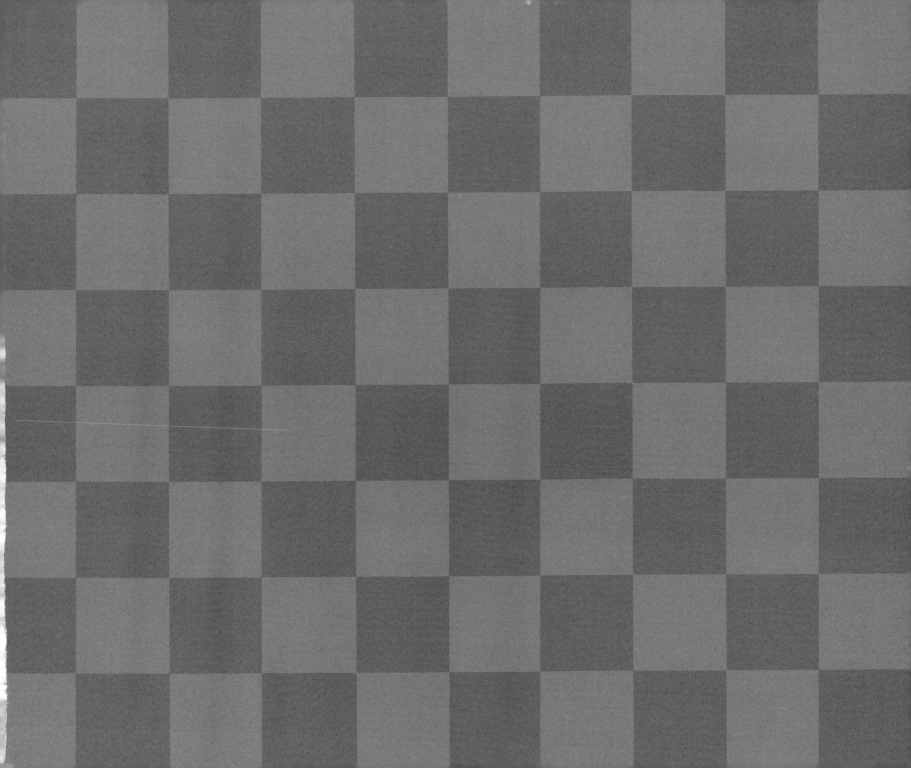